SOMETHING NEW
FOR A BEAR TO DO
Adventures of Mr Manders and Edward James

SHIRLEY ISHERWOOD
Something New for a Bear to do

Illustrated by David McKee

HUTCHINSON

London   Melbourne   Auckland   Johannesburg

First published in 1986 by Hutchinson Children's Books Ltd
An imprint of Century Hutchinson Ltd
Brookmount House, 62–65 Chandos Place, Covent Garden,
London WC2N 4NW

Century Hutchinson Publishing Group (Australia) Pty Ltd
16–22 Church Street, Hawthorn, Melbourne, Victoria 3122

Century Hutchinson Group (NZ) Ltd
32–34 View Road, PO Box 40-086, Glenfield, Auckland 10

Century Hutchinson Group, (SA) Pty Ltd
PO Box 337, Bergvlei 2012, South Africa

Set in Baskerville by BookEns, Saffron Walden, Essex

Printed and bound in Great Britain by
Anchor Brandon Ltd, Tiptree, Essex

British Library Cataloguing in Publication Data
Isherwood, Shirley
Something new for a bear to do.
I. Title
823'.914[J]   PZ7

ISBN 0-09-163340-0

Contents

For Michael Richard Edwin Vanes

Something New
for a Bear to Do

One morning, Mr Manders woke with an interesting thought in his head. He woke the little bear, Edward James, to tell him about it. 'It is this,' said Mr Manders. 'Why do bears always do the things that bears do? Why don't they do other things?'

Edward James said that he didn't know. He wanted to go back to sleep, but Mr Manders took him by the paw, and led him out into the garden, to discuss the matter further.

It was very early in the morning. The garden was full of mist, and the birds were waking up, and singing in the branches of the trees. 'That is what I mean,' said Mr Manders. 'Why do birds sing so beautifully in the trees, and bears don't?'

He climbed a tree, sat down on a branch and began to sing. His voice was very deep and low. 'OO-ROO-OO-ROW,' he sang – then he looked down at Edward James. 'How did I sound?' he asked.

'Like a bear singing in a tree,' said Edward James.

Mr Manders sighed. He came down from the tree, and together he and Edward James went on through the garden, to where a little stream ran over stones and pebbles. As they drew near, a frog jumped from the grass and into the water.

'Now that is something that bears don't often do,' said Mr Manders – and straight away he took a deep breath, flung himself forwards, and sat down in the water. Then he sighed, and climbed out again.

'And the reason they *don't* do it', he said, as he sat by Edward James's side, 'is, it isn't very interesting.'

He lay down, and after a time the sun came out, his fur began to dry, and a little cloud of steam rose from his wet tummy.

As Mr Manders lay there gently steaming, a party of ants went by – each ant carrying a scrap of straw, or a tiny ball of earth. 'Now that *is* interesting,' said Mr Manders. 'They are working – building – and a bear could do that!'

He got up, and as Edward James watched, he began to collect stones and twigs. He picked them up, and carried them across the garden, and put them down – just as the ants had done. Very soon he had built a little heap of stones and twigs, and he stood there gazing at it.

'What is it?' asked Edward James.

'It's plain to see what it is,' said Mr Manders. 'It's a sort of . . . .'

'Well, I'm not sure what it is,' he said, as he and Edward James climbed through the gap in the fence. 'But it must be *something*.' They crossed the field, lay down beneath the hedge, and very soon fell asleep.

When Mr Manders woke he found a spider dangling over his face, on the end of a long fine thread. As Mr Manders watched, the spider ran up and down the thread, like a little yo-yo on the end of a piece of string.

'Now that is a nice new thing for a bear to do,' said Mr Manders, and he searched beneath the hedge until he found an old piece of string.

'I shall go up and down,' he said, as he climbed a tree and tied the end of the string to a branch. Then he tied the other end of the string to his tummy, and jumped.

'Or not,' he said, as he hung in the air above Edward James's head.

He began to scrabble about wildly, but this only made him spin round and round.

'You see, Edward James,' he said, when at last he stopped spinning, 'one needs a lot of legs to go up and down – and I've only got two.'

The string broke, and he fell into the soft grass. Sadly, he picked himself up. 'I can't seem to do any new thing at all,' he said.

They began to make their way back home, but stopped for a time by the side of the pond, to watch the little water boatman rowing himself across the water.

The sight was so cheering that Mr Manders climbed on to the garden fence, and began to sing. He had never sung on the garden fence before, and he enjoyed it immensely. 'Row, row, row your boat, gently down the stream!' he sang, in his delightfully deep voice. 'Merrily, merrily, merrily, merrily, life is but a dream!'

'How was that?' he asked, when the song was ended.

'Like a bear singing on a fence,' said Edward James. 'A bear singing *beautifully* on a fence,' he added.

So with that, they both went home for breakfast.

An Extraordinary Happening

One morning, Mr Manders woke up with the feeling that something extraordinary was going to happen. It was the kind of feeling he got when he woke up on his birthday. He didn't think it *was* his birthday – but just to make sure he went down the hall, to see if there were any birthday cards with 'Happy birthday Mr Manders!' written on them. There was nothing at all on the door-mat, so Mr Manders went back and woke up the little bear, Edward James.

'Perhaps the postman hasn't been yet,' said Edward James. So Mr Manders propped the front door open with a large stone, and he and Edward James sat on a stool and waited for the postman to arrive.

13

As they sat, a delightful spring breeze blew from the garden, together with the sound of singing birds. There was a great feeling of excitement in the air.

'Perhaps it's nothing at all to do with birthdays,' said Mr Manders. 'Perhaps it's an extraordinary thing which is going to happen in the garden.'

He got down from the stool, and trotted along the path. 'I hope it doesn't happen before I get to it,' he said as he went. 'Hurry up, Edward James, or you might miss it!'

But Edward James was still sitting on the stool in the doorway. 'It might happen here,' he said. 'And then *you* would miss it.'

'You're right!' said Mr Manders, and he sat down with a thump.

The thump woke up a family of fieldmice. They woke with a start, and with the feeling that something extraordinary was about to happen. They crept to the edge of the long grass, and saw Mr Manders sitting with his chin in his paw. Some of the older mice thought that this was quite an ordinary sight – for they had seen Mr Manders before. But the younger mice had never seen a large bear sitting in the path before, and they found the sight quite extraordinary. 'Look at his ears – look at his paws – look at his wonderful nose!' they said.

But Mr Manders heard and saw nothing. He was busy thinking. He thought, the extraordinary thing could happen here, where I am sitting; or, it might happen there, where Edward James is sitting; or, he said to himself, it *could* happen somewhere else altogether!

He got up, and trotted down the path, looking round to see if he could find a place where something extraordinary might happen.

The fieldmice got up too and ran after him. They ran as fast as they could, but Mr Manders took such long strides that soon he was lost to sight, round the bend in the path. At this, some of the youngest mice sat down and began to cry. But the older mice pulled them back on to their feet, wiped their eyes and noses, and hurried them off, along a short cut across the garden.

While the mice were making their way across the garden, Mr Manders was trotting along the path, which led in a circle right round the garden. Because he was going in a circle, he very soon came back to the place he had started from. The mice caught up with him, just as he reached it, and everyone sat down, and wondered what was going to happen next.

'I could run round again,' said Mr Manders. 'But you see, Edward James, whatever it is that is going to happen might happen round the bend before I get to it – then I wouldn't see it. Or it might happen in a place I've just run past – then it would happen behind me, and I wouldn't see it.'

He put his chin in his paw again, and wondered if it would make any difference if he ran very quickly. 'Some things take a long time to happen,' he said. 'So if I ran very quickly, even if it happened behind me, it would still be happening when I came round again, and I would see it. Wouldn't I?'

Edward James said that he didn't know; but Mr Manders decided that he would try anyway, and he set off at a furious pace. The mice jumped to their feet and ran after him. Some of them thought that it was a race, and that they must stay on the path. But others thought that it was a game, and that they were to catch Mr Manders in any way that they could. They rushed across the garden, taking the short cut. Then, squealing happily, they dashed out, tripped him up, and sent him bowling head over heels into a flowerbed.

Edward James sat in the doorway, and watched the racing mice go down the path and round the bend. How extraordinary, he thought, and jumped down from the stool and went along the path to Mr Manders.

Mr Manders picked himself up from the flowerbed, and looked at the row of bright little faces. How extraordinary, he thought. How very extraordinary – to be tripped up by mice!

He stood for a moment, looking round the garden. Then, as nothing else extraordinary seemed to be happening, he brushed the dust from his paws and tummy, and he and Edward James went back into the house for breakfast.

Travelling Bear

One morning, Mr Manders had a wonderful idea. He went to tell the little bear all about it. 'Travel!' he said. 'That is what we should do, Edward James! Explore new places! See new faces!'

'Where shall we go?' asked Edward James.

'Anywhere!' said Mr Manders.

'When?' asked Edward James, who was hungry and wanted to eat his breakfast.

'Now,' said Mr Manders. 'At once!' He flung open the door, and stood sniffing the air. 'That is the best way to travel!' he said. 'To just get up and go!'

He strode off down the path. Edward James wrapped up his breakfast, and ran out after him.

But by the time he reached the gap in the fence Mr Manders was already crossing the field, and was hidden by the long grass. Edward James heard him singing as he went. Then the sound grew fainter, and fainter, until it couldn't be heard at all.

'Has he gone to the left or gone to the right,' said Edward James, 'or has he gone straight ahead?'

There was no way of knowing, so he sat down, and unwrapped his breakfast – three marmite sandwiches and a chocolate biscuit. He set it out carefully on the greaseproof paper – and he was just about to start eating when he heard the sound of Mr Manders singing once more. Louder and louder came the sound, until at last Mr Manders himself came striding out from the long grass. He seemed surprised to see Edward James.

'It's a funny thing about travelling,' he said. 'Sometimes you think you're going somewhere, but really you're just coming back again.'

He took a sandwich, in an absent-minded way, and set off once more. Edward James wrapped up the rest of his breakfast; but by the time he had finished, Mr Manders had disappeared again.

'Has he gone to the left or gone to the right,' said Edward James, 'or has he gone straight ahead?' It was impossible to tell. So he sat down and unwrapped his breakfast again.

He had eaten only half a sandwich, when Mr Manders reappeared. He came suddenly from the long grass, and he looked puzzled.

'I meant to go in a straight line,' he said, as he took a sandwich, 'but I seem to keep turning corners.'

He sounded rather discouraged, and Edward James wondered what he could do to cheer him up.

'Perhaps we should go home,' he said.

'Certainly not,' said Mr Manders. 'When a bear wants to go somewhere, he must *go* somewhere!' And he set off immediately, with his half-eaten sandwich in his paw.

Edward James sat and wondered if he should wrap his breakfast up again – or not. Before he could decide, he heard Mr Manders calling to him from the long grass.

'Help!' he shouted. 'Where am I?'

Edward James ran to find him – but Mr Manders was nowhere to be found. There was nothing but the sound of his voice, calling from different parts of the field. On and on ran Edward James, following the sound of Mr Manders's voice. Am I going left, or right, he wondered as he ran, or am I going straight ahead?

Then, suddenly, he came upon his breakfast lying forlornly in the grass, and knew that he had run in a circle.

So, off he went again – and the next time he came back to his breakfast Mr Manders was sitting beside it, eating the last of the sandwiches.

'This travelling has been a great disappointment to me,' he said, as he broke off a piece of sandwich and gave it to Edward James. 'I haven't seen one new place, or one new face – all I've seen is grass.' He lay back, folded his paws over his tummy, and went to sleep.

Edward James sat and ate his piece of sandwich. Then, what with the travelling, and the excitement, and the rushing through the long grass looking for Mr Manders, he thought that he was feeling a little tired himself. 'I'll have a little nap,' he said, 'and save the chocolate biscuit for later.'

When he opened his eyes again, he found a face peering at him from between the blades of grass – a furry face with two bright eyes and sharp white teeth. Between the teeth was Edward James's biscuit.

Edward James sighed, and folded up the greaseproof paper. He folded it carefully into a little square. Then he woke Mr Manders, and together they made their way home.

'This is the nicest part of travelling!' said Mr Manders. 'Climbing through your own gap in the fence! Going back to your own home!'

'And eating your own breakfast,' said Edward James.

Locked Out

One night, just as Mr Manders was going to sleep, he heard a little voice calling to him from the garden.

'Help!' it said. 'I'm locked outside!'

Mr Manders hurried to the door, stood on a stool and looked through the letter box. The little bear, Edward James, was standing on the doorstep.

'I'm locked out!' he said.

Mr Manders went to look for the key to unlock the door – but it was nowhere to be found. He put his paw through the letter box, to pull Edward James inside. But Edward James was too far down to be reached.

'You'll have to stand on something,' said Mr

Manders. So Edward James brought a large stone from the garden. But even when he stood on a stone, he was still a long way from the letter box.

Mr Manders hurried to the kitchen, and came back with a big ball of string. 'Tie the end round your tummy,' he said, as he pushed a length of the string through the letter box. 'Tie it tightly, and I'll pull you in.'

Edward James took hold of the end of the string, and wound it round his tummy. Then he began to look for the other end, so that he could tie a bow.

'Stop!' cried Mr Manders, as the ball of string grew smaller and smaller. But Edward James just went on pulling until at last the string disappeared and the letter box closed with a *click*.

Mr Manders opened the letter box and looked out. Edward James was standing on the doorstep, in a great tangle of string. 'What do I do now?' he asked.

'I'll have to think about it,' said Mr Manders. He sat down on the stool, put his chin in his paw, and thought as hard as he could. But he couldn't think of a way to get a small bear through a letter box.

'I'm cold,' came the voice of Edward James from the doorstep.

So Mr Manders brought his blue blanket, and pushed it through the letter box. Then he sat down, and began to think again. But he had hardly had one thought, when he heard the voice of Edward James once more.

'I'm hungry!' he said.

So Mr Manders went to the kitchen, and brought a biscuit, and pushed it through the letter box.

'Thank you,' said Edward James.

'You're welcome,' said Mr Manders, 'but please don't interrupt again. I'm trying to think of a way to get you through the letter box.'

He sat down on the stool again, put his chin in his paw, and closed his eyes. But he still couldn't think of a way.

Crunch-crunch-crunch, went Edward James, eating his biscuit on the door step. Then – 'I'm frightened,' he said.

Mr Manders opened the letter box, and looked at him; he seemed very small and lonely, standing there in his blue blanket and his tangle of string. Mr Manders tried to think of something bracing to say – some rousing words which would make a small bear feel bolder. 'You're a bear!' he said. 'Pull your socks up!'

Edward James sat down on the doorstep. He felt rather puzzled. He knew that he was a bear, and he wondered why pulling his socks up would make him feel braver – even if he were wearing his socks – which he wasn't.

'My feet are cold,' he said. 'Please may I have my socks?'

Mr Manders sighed, brought Edward James's

socks, and pushed them through the letter box.

'Thank you,' said Edward James.

Mr Manders sat down, and began to think again. After thinking a great deal on the matter, he said to himself: 'I have come to the conclusion that the best way to get a small bear through a letter box is . . . .' And there the thought ended, which was disappointing as it was the longest thought he had had.

Outside, it began to rain. Soon Edward James found that he was sitting in a puddle. His bottom was wet, and he began to sneeze. 'NISHY!' he said.

Mr Manders stood on the stool, opened the letter box, and looked out. The doorstep was empty, and there was nothing to be seen but the dark, wet garden. 'Edward James, where are you?' he called.

'Here,' said Edward James. Mr Manders turned, and saw him coming down the hall, trailing the wet blanket and the string behind him. 'I came in through the cat-flap!' he said happily.

When Edward James was asleep, Mr Manders sat down on the stool, and put his chin in his paw. He felt that he had been foolish not to have remembered the cat-flap, which was just the right size for a small bear to climb through. 'I'm not a clever bear,' he said to himself, as he sat. 'Not what you would call a *bright* bear.'

Then he thought that, after all, his idea about the string had been a good idea if only Edward James had understood it. And with this happy thought, he went back to bed, and slept soundly until morning.

The Birthday Party

One afternoon, when Mr Manders was walking in the garden, he heard a voice say, 'Oh, it's my birthday.' It was a very quiet and gentle little voice, and for a moment, Mr Manders wondered if he had really heard it – but then it came again. 'It's my birthday!' it said.

Mr Manders was surprised. He was alone in the garden. The little bear, Edward James, was in the house, having his afternoon nap. But just to make sure, Mr Manders went to look; and there he was, lying fast asleep, with his bottom in the air. Mr Manders crept out of the house, and went back to the garden.

'Oh, it's my birthday,' said the voice again. Mr Manders wondered who it could belong to. He sat down on a little hill, and thought of everyone he knew – but no one he knew had a quiet, gentle voice. Mr Manders got up, and trotted back to the house, where Edward James was just waking up.

'It's someone's birthday,' he said, 'but I don't know whose.'

'Many happy returns,' said Edward James, who was still half-asleep.

'It isn't *my* birthday,' said Mr Manders. 'That is the problem.' He took the little bear by the paw, and led him out into the garden. 'If we don't know whose birthday it is,' he said, 'how can we go to the party? We don't know where it is, or when it begins.'

'Perhaps if we sit quietly, and listen, we will hear it begin,' said Edward James.

Mr Manders thought that this was a good idea. So he and Edward James sat quietly, and listened. They sat for a long time, but heard nothing at all – only the sound of the bees buzzing around the flowers. The sun began to go down, and the garden grew dark.

'If the party doesn't start soon,' said Mr Manders, 'it will be too late.' He put his paw to the side of this mouth, and shouted. 'Hello there! Hadn't you better begin!'

But there was no answer.

'Perhaps we'd better start the party ourselves,'

said Mr Manders, 'as a sort of a hint – in case they've forgotten.'

Edward James didn't think that anyone would forget their own birthday party, but he trotted into the house with Mr Manders, where they found an old squeaker, and a balloon left over from Edward James's last birthday.

Back in the garden, Edward James blew the squeaker, and Mr Manders blew up the balloon and tied it to a branch of a tree. It looked rather lonely hanging there by itself, so Mr Manders and Edward James went back to the house, and found two more balloons, and some tinsel left over from Christmas.

The tree looked very pretty when they had finished decorating it, and Mr Manders and Edward James sat down on the little hill to admire it. As they sat, the voice came again. 'My birthday,' it said.

Edward James thought that the voice came from the hill, but Mr Manders just said, 'Don't be silly, hills don't have birthdays. It's the birthday of someone too shy to come out and enjoy themselves.'

He went to the middle of the garden, and shouted as loudly as he could. 'Come and have your party!' But no one came.

Mr Manders went back to where Edward James sat with his squeaker. 'I think they just need a bit more encouragement,' he said. So he and Edward James went back to the house, and brought out Edward James's gramophone, and his record of 'Waltzing Matilda'.

It was a very old record, and sometimes the needle got stuck. But once the music started, it made them feel like dancing. They danced until they were hungry; then they went back to the house, and brought out some honey sandwiches and a fruit cake – which they had been saving for Sunday. They also brought a candle for the cake. It was a large, ordinary candle – there being no birthday candles left. But it looked lovely on the cake, and it lit up the dark garden wonderfully.

'It's a very good party,' said Mr Manders, as he and Edward James ate some of the sandwiches and the cake. 'I'm glad we didn't miss it!' Then, because it was very late, and past Edward James's

bedtime, they went back to the house and climbed into bed.

But Edward James couldn't sleep for wondering whose birthday party it had been. He climbed from his bed and sat down on the windowsill, and stared out at the garden, where the sky was full of stars and the candle still burned on the cake. As he watched he saw the mole come from his burrow under the little hill, followed by all his friends and relations. 'Mr Manders!' said Edward James. 'I know whose birthday party it is.'

But Mr Manders was fast asleep. He slept through the noise of the party games, and the sound of the guests singing 'Happy birthday to you!' He slept through the sound of the gramophone – even though the needle got stuck in the record again, and, 'Waltzing . . . Waltzing . . . Waltzing,' it said; until the party ended, the stars went out, and the candle flame flickered and died.

The Boat

All through the winter, Mr Manders talked about building a boat. 'As soon as springtime comes,' he said, 'we'll build our boat, we'll set our sail, and sail across the pond.'

Edward James felt that he couldn't wait! Every morning he and Mr Manders walked through the garden, through the gap in the fence, and across the field to look at the pond. As they went, they talked about their boat, and about how beautiful it would be. 'Shall we paint it white, or blue?' said Mr Manders. Edward James couldn't decide which colour he liked best – but it didn't matter; there was plenty of time in which to choose. And then, quite suddenly one morning, it was Spring. 'It's time to begin!' said Mr Manders.

Together they loaded the wood on to the barrow, and wheeled it across the field to the pond. Then Mr Manders sent Edward James back to the house, for the hammer and the bag of nails. 'I hope he lets me knock in some of the nails,' said Edward James as he went. But when he returned, Mr Manders just sent him back again, for a measure and a piece of chalk.

All day long Mr Manders built the boat, and Edward James went back and forth, bringing things – a bigger hammer, more nails and some pincers to take the nails out again when they went in crooked. Mr Manders sang as he worked. 'Oh, we'll build our boat, we'll set our sail, we'll sail across the pond!'

The next day was just the same. Bang-bang-bang went Mr Manders with the hammer – and back and forth went Edward James. He brought a shady hat for when the sun grew too hot for Mr Manders, he brought a jug of cooling lemonade, a brush to sweep up the wood shavings and a bag to put the shavings in. He looked for the hammer when Mr Manders mislaid it in the grass, and he collected all the crooked nails, in case they should ever come in useful.

'I want to knock in some nails,' he said, from time to time. But Mr Manders didn't seem to hear him.

'Oh, we'll build our boat, we'll set our sail, we'll sail across the pond!' he sang.

The days went by, the boat grew bigger and Edward James's legs grew more tired. At the end of a long and tiring afternoon, he went back to the garden and sat down beneath a tree. As he sat he could hear Mr Manders singing as he worked.

'It isn't our boat any more,' said Edward James. 'It's *his* boat. I haven't knocked in one nail!'

Edward James stayed in the garden. When evening came he saw the light of the lantern shining in the field, and the black shape of Mr Manders, as he trotted to and fro building the boat.

Edward James got up, and went across the field. 'I haven't knocked in one nail!' he said angrily.

'Oh, Edward James,' said Mr Manders, 'I'm sorry!' He held out the last nail, and Edward James took the hammer and knocked the nail in.

'But I still can't decide what colour the boat should be,' said Mr Manders. He sat down, dejectedly, by the two pots of paint. 'You choose, Edward James,' he said.

'Blue,' said Edward James. 'The boat should be blue!'

He took the brush, and began to paint. He painted bits of himself, and bits of Mr Manders by accident – but it didn't matter. He painted all night, by the light of the lantern and the moon. Then, in the morning, when the sun came up and the paint was dry, he and Mr Manders pushed the boat out on to the water, set the sail, and sailed away over the pond.

The Kite

In January, it snowed; in February, it rained; but in March, the March winds blew. 'It's time to fly our kite!' said Mr Manders. He went to the shed, with Edward James, and together they searched amongst the seed boxes and old sacks, until they found the kite.

But it was an old kite; there were tears in it, and half of the tail was missing. Mr Manders went into the garden to make a new kite – a bright red kite, with a magnificent tail. When it was finished, he and Edward James took it out to the field. Then Edward James took hold of the kite-string, and began to run.

But Edward James was a very small bear, and the kite was a very large kite. The wind blew it this way and that, and Edward James staggered along behind it.

'Let me help you,' said Mr Manders.

'No,' said Edward James, and he set off once more. The wind blew him round and round, then backwards and forwards – but still he clung to the kite-string.

Mr Manders watched for a time, then he lay back, folded his paws over his tummy, and closed his eyes. A moment later, Edward James said, 'Look! I'm flying!'

'Don't be silly,' said Mr Manders. 'Bears can't fly.' But when he opened his eyes, he saw that Edward James was hanging some inches above his head.

'Come down at once!' said Mr Manders; but as he spoke the wind carried the kite and Edward James across the field.

'I'm flying – I'm flying!' he shouted as he went. And so he was, and there was nothing that Mr Manders could do about it. He ran after Edward James, and jumped up and tried to grab his feet. But Edward James just rose up in the air, out of reach.

'Did you do that on purpose?' said Mr Manders.

'No,' said Edward James, 'the wind did it.' But he looked quite pleased to be doing something that he shouldn't be doing – and to be able to say, quite truthfully, that he wasn't doing it on purpose. 'It just happened,' he shouted, as he was whisked off over the field once more.

That's all very well, thought Mr Manders, as he watched Edward James bobbing about in the gusty wind, but what will happen if the wind starts blowing in just one direction? Suppose it blows south – he'll end up in Africa!

But the wind seemed content just to blow this way and that, and Edward James drifted about the field, giggling.

It's all very well giggling, thought Mr Manders. But what happens if the wind stops suddenly? He'll come crashing down to earth! He turned and ran back to the house, and brought out a big, fat cushion. At least he'll have somewhere soft to fall, he thought, as he put the cushion down in the middle of the field.

But suppose he doesn't fall in the middle of the field!

He picked up the cushion, and, holding it tightly in both arms, ran to where Edward James was hovering in the air. 'Come down now!' said Mr Manders. 'Come down on to the cushion!'

But Edward James just said, 'Can't!' and floated off once more.

There's nothing I can do but follow him, thought Mr Manders. With a sigh, he picked up the cushion, and began to run round the field.

For the rest of the afternoon, Edward James sailed over the field, and Mr Manders ran after him with the cushion. He ran until his legs would carry him no further, then he sank down flat on to the cushion, and stared up at the evening sky.

Above his head, Edward James bobbed up and down on the end of the kite-string. Then the wind began to die, and he began to come down. Inch by inch he dropped until he landed gently – FLUMP! – on Mr Manders's tummy.

'Nice of you to drop by,' said Mr Manders. He wound up the kite-string, and together he and Edward James went back to the house. 'Don't do it again!' said Mr Manders. But when Edward James had gone to sleep, he looked at the kite standing in a corner of the kitchen; and he listened to the wind, which had risen again, and was blowing gustily over the field; then he took up the kite, and crept quietly out into the garden. After all, he thought, it *did* look a lot of fun!

But Mr Manders was much heavier than Edward James. No matter how quickly he ran, or how strongly the wind blew, his feet wouldn't leave the ground. He sat down and unwound some more of the kite-string, and let the kite soar up alone. I always knew bears couldn't fly, thought Mr Manders.

Well, *some* bears can't fly.

How to Cure
Hiccups

One morning Edward James woke up with hiccups. He hiccupped all through breakfast, and he hiccupped all through the walk across the field.

'Hold your breath, and count to ten,' said Mr Manders. So Edward James held his breath. He held it for so long that Mr Manders became alarmed. 'Start breathing again!' he said.

'Hic!' said Edward James. He was a little cross, as he didn't see how he could count to ten while he was holding his breath. 'How can I talk without breathing?' he said.

'I'll count for you,' said Mr Manders. So Edward James held his breath again, and Mr Manders began to count.

'One – two – three – four – five – six,' he said, looking at Edward James, and thinking that perhaps it was a dangerous thing to do, to hold one's breath for so long. 'Seveneightnineten!' he said.

Edward James let out his breath.

'How do you feel?' asked Mr Manders.

'Hic!' said Edward James.

Mr Manders hurried to the house, and took out his book of remedies, and looked under 'H' for hiccups. 'To cure hiccups', said the book, 'try giving the patient a fright.'

He went back to the garden, where Edward James was sitting under a tree. 'BOO' said Mr Manders, jumping out from behind the tree.

'Boo to you too,' said Edward James. 'Hic!'

Mr Manders went to have another look at the book. 'If a sudden fright fails to cure,' he read, 'drop a small cold object – perhaps a door key – down the patient's clothing.'

He hurried to the front door and took the key from the lock. But as he trotted across the garden with the key in his paw, he thought, Edward James doesn't wear clothes – except for socks when his feet are cold. He doesn't need clothes, he's covered in fur. But the book says I have to drop a key down his clothes. So the only thing to do is to find him something to wear.

He went back to the house and got out the tablecloth, and hurried back to the garden.

Edward James was surprised to find himself suddenly wearing the tablecloth.

'It's to cure your hiccups,' said Mr Manders.

'Hic?' said Edward James.

'And now', said Mr Manders, 'I drop this cold key down your back.'

But the key wasn't cold. It was quite warm from being held in Mr Manders's paw. Mr Manders hurried to the stream, and dangled the key in the water. When it was nice and cold, he went back to the garden. But Edward James was no longer sitting under the tree.

'Where are you?' called Mr Manders – but there was no answer.

Mr Manders looked everywhere for Edward James – and at last he found him wandering dejectedly about the field in his tablecloth. Mr Manders took him by the paw and led him to the stream. 'Stay there!' he said firmly. 'I'll soon cure your hiccups!'

He dangled the key in the water and swished it to and fro. After such a busy time, it was pleasant to sit and listen to the gentle sound of the water; and he had almost fallen asleep, when, 'HIC!' said Edward James suddenly in his ear. The noise startled Mr Manders so much that he let go of the key, and it dropped down between the stones and pebbles at the bottom of the stream.

With a sigh, Mr Manders waded into the water. Edward James scrambled down from the bank to help him. Together they lifted up a great many stones and pebbles, until at last they found the key, sticking in the mud.

Tired and wet, they went back to the garden. Edward James sat down beneath the tree once more. His paws were covered in mud, and his tablecloth was stained with waterweed and grass. He looked so funny that Mr Manders began to laugh. He laughed so much that he had to lie down for a little while. When he caught his breath again, he stood up and held out the key. 'Now I'll put it down your back, and cure your hiccups,' he said.

'I haven't got them any more,' said Edward James.

Mr Manders stood quietly and listened; there wasn't a hiccup to be heard. 'Thank goodness for that!' he said. He bundled up the tablecloth, and together he and Edward James began to make their way back to the house.

'What's for lunch?' asked Edward James, as they went.

'Boiled eggs,' said Mr Manders. 'Boiled eggs, and – HIC!'

So Edward James wrapped him in the wet tablecloth, and dropped the key down his back.

Changes

Mr Manders and Edward James lived in the house by the stream. They had lived there happily for some time, when one day a small furry creature came down the path, carrying a large flowered bag. She said that her name was Florence, but what kind of a creature she was it was impossible to tell, and neither Mr Manders nor Edward James thought it polite to ask.

'Please may I live in the summer house at the bottom of the garden?' she said. 'I am very tidy in my habits, and I like to keep myself *to* myself.'

Edward James liked her at once. Her eyes were round and bright, and her paws were like little hands. But Mr Manders wasn't sure that he would like someone living in his summer house.

(It was a pleasant little house, painted white and made of wood. He often thought that he would sit there on summer evenings but somehow he never got round to it.)

Mr Manders went for a walk with Edward James, to help him make up his mind. Florence followed them, and sat down on her bag in the middle of the field. 'I won't be any trouble,' she said. 'I don't give parties, and I don't play any loud musical instruments – I would certainly never consider the bagpipes.'

'Please let her stay,' said Edward James.

Mr Manders sighed. 'Someone new always wants to change things,' he said. 'They say "Oh, I always have toast for tea on *Thursdays*," or "I think Friday is a much better day for winding the clock." ' He took Edward James's paw, and began to walk faster and faster as he thought of all the changes there might be if he let Florence stay. 'They find fault with your field,' he said, 'or they want to dig up your begonias, and plant snapdragons instead.'

'I *hate* snapdragons!' he shouted – and walked so quickly that Edward James's feet left the ground and he took six steps in the air.

'I want Florence to stay!' said Edward James, and he pulled his paw free and threw himself down on the ground. Mr Manders bent to pick him up, but Edward James made himself very

heavy – which was an interesting trick he did from time to time.

'Please get up,' said Mr Manders.

'No!' said Edward James.

Mr Manders sat down beside him. 'It's just that I like things to stay the same,' he said. 'It's a nice, comfortable feeling when things stay the same.' But Edward James just glared up at him from the grass.

'When things change, it's like this,' said Mr Manders. 'You go out into the garden and it's just the same as it always is, and you go and look at the stream, and that's just the same; and then you go through the gap in the fence, and suddenly, everything's not the same. There's a Florence in your field.'

'I *want* a Florence in my field!' shouted Edward James, and he got up and ran off through the long grass. Mr Manders ran after him, but Edward James just shouted, 'Go away! I don't like you any more!'

Mr Manders went to sit down at the side of the field. Edward James sat on the other side – and Florence continued to sit in the middle. And so they sat, the three of them, until the sun went down.

Everything's changed, thought Mr Manders. We should be making toast for tea in a friendly way, just as we always do. One change makes another change happen – I must try to stop them, before there are any more!

He got up, and went to where Florence sat on her bag. 'You may stay,' he said. 'But I don't want any more changes. We *always* have toast for tea on Monday. I *always* wind the clock on Tuesday. And I *hate* snapdragons.'

'I wasn't thinking of planting any,' said Florence. (In a rather sharp way, Mr Manders thought.)

When Florence was settled in the summer house, Mr Manders and Edward James went for another walk. Everything was as it always was – garden, stream and field were just the same. But when at last they made their way home for tea, they found a treacle tart on the windowsill. It was covered with a little white starched cloth, and pinned to the cloth was a note. 'I *always* make treacle tart on Monday. Yours Respectfully, Florence.'

'Well,' said Mr Manders, as he carried the tart into the kitchen, 'it doesn't seem to have been a bad change.'

'In fact,' he said, some time later, licking his sticky paws, 'it's been a quite satisfactory change – as changes go.'

The Balloonists

One morning, Mr Manders woke with a strange and restless feeling. No matter how hard he thought about it, he couldn't decide what it was he wanted to do. First he decided that he would like to visit Florence. So he brushed his jacket, smiled at himself in the hall mirror, and set off down the path with a jaunty step. But half way down the path he began to walk slower and slower, until at last he stopped. 'This isn't what I want to do,' he said.

He went back to the house, and hung up his jacket. Perhaps what I really want to do is plant some begonias, he thought. So he got out his trowel, and went out into the garden once more. But as soon as he knelt by the flowerbed, he knew that planting begonias wasn't what he really wanted to do.

'Perhaps what you really want to do is clear out the attic,' said Edward James. So together they climbed the attic stairs, flung open the door, and went inside. The attic was full of dusty bundles and boxes. Mr Manders looked at them.

'This isn't what I want to do,' he said. 'What I want is not to be a boring bear who plants begonias and clears out the attic.'

But Edward James wasn't listening. He was unwrapping a huge parcel which stood in the middle of the attic floor. First, a wicker basket came into view, with strong white ropes tied round the edges. And then a great balloon, folded up neatly, and painted with suns and moons and stars. It was the hot air balloon which had belonged to Mr Manders's great-uncle, Darcy Manders.

Mr Manders and Edward James dragged the
balloon down the stairs, across the garden, and
out into the field. Mr Manders was very excited.
'I think this is what I really want to do,' he said, as
they spread the balloon out in the grass. He lit
the burner, and the flames roared out with a
WHOOSH. The balloon began to fill with hot
air. When it was full and round, and bobbing
about in the breeze, Mr Manders climbed into
the basket.

Edward James scrambled up after him. 'Are you sure it's what you want to do?' he asked.

'I think so,' said Mr Manders. 'But sometimes you can't be sure if a thing's what you want to do, until you actually do it.'

He threw out the heavy bags of ballast (which were weighting the balloon down, on to the ground), and the balloon began to rise. Florence came running over the field to wave goodbye. Edward James looked over the edge of the basket, and watched as she grew smaller and smaller. Then the field itself began to shrink, until he could see the fields beyond, and far away in the distance a misty blue line, which was the sea.

'Is it what you want to do?' he asked Mr Manders.

'Yes, it is,' said Mr Manders. 'I'm quite sure of it. In fact,' he said, as they suddenly floated sideways and upwards, 'this is all I shall ever want to do. To see the world! To be here today and gone tomorrow!'

He turned up the burner, and gave the balloon a burst of hot air which sent it whisking over villages, and church spires, and country lanes – where bands of hikers stopped and cried, 'Look! Two bears in a balloon!'

Mr Manders was very pleased. He waved to the hikers, and cried, 'No more begonias!' (Which puzzled them a little).

But Edward James was getting hungry. He didn't know what time it was, but it felt like lunch time. So Mr Manders turned off the burner, and slowly the balloon sank down on to the beach. They had reached the end of the land. There was nothing in front of them but the sea.

Mr Manders and Edward James had never seen the sea; and for a time they just stood and stared at it, and listened to the sound of the waves breaking on the shore.

'There's no one here but us,' said Mr Manders. 'We have discovered this place.'

He wrote 'Manders Beach' in the sand with his paw. Then he and Edward James sat in silence, and watched as the waves crept nearer and nearer and the words were washed away.

'The sea is very beautiful,' said Mr Manders at last.

'It is also very big,' said Edward James.

'But there's another land on the other side!' cried Mr Manders, and he jumped to his feet and brushed the sand from his paws.

'Do you want to find it?' said Edward James. 'Is that really what you want to do?'

'No,' said Mr Manders. 'What I really want to do is go home.'

'So do I,' said Edward James.

Florence was waiting for them when at last they sailed back over the chimneys of the house.

She was sitting in the middle of the field, with her paws folded neatly in her lap. Edward James saw her as he peered over the edge of the basket. He saw too the bright begonia beds, the white roof of the summer house, and the little stream like a silver ribbon, running at the bottom of the garden.

They left the balloon in the field, climbed back through the gap in the fence, and went into the kitchen. The fire burned brightly in the little iron stove, and because it was Monday there was a treacle tart on the windowsill.

'Everything is just the same,' said Mr Manders happily.

But everything was not the same, and would never be again. For now they were bears who had travelled. They were bears who had gone forth into the world. They were bears who had seen the sea.

The Snowball

One morning, when Edward James woke up, he found that it had been snowing in the night. So he decided that he would go out into the garden and make a snowman – a beautiful white snowman who would stand as long as the cold weather lasted. He would be there in the morning, glistening in the sunlight, and at night he would gleam in the moonlight, like a marble statue.

As soon as he had eaten his breakfast, Edward James ran outside – but he had scarcely made the round fat body of the snowman, when Mr Manders came by.

'Aha!' he said. 'A giant snowball. I used to make giant snowballs when *I* was a small bear.'

'It isn't a snowball,' said Edward James. 'It's a snowman.'

But Mr Manders wasn't listening; he was walking round and round the body of the snowman, and prodding it with his paw.

'It's not really what you'd call a *giant* snowball, is it?' he said. Then, before Edward James could stop him, he pushed the snowman over, and began to trundle him down the path.

Edward James stood and watched as Mr Manders disappeared round the bend in the path, pushing the snowball before him. In a short time he reappeared, a little out of breath. The snowball was much bigger.

'Do you understand what is happening?' he asked, as he plodded past Edward James. 'Each time the snowball rolls round, it gathers up more snow. And that,' he said, as he vanished round the bend of the path once more, 'is how you make a giant snowball.'

It was some time before Edward James saw the giant snowball again, but at last it rolled slowly into view, and came to a halt before the doorstep.

'It's enormous!' said Edward James.

'Enormous?' said Mr Manders. 'Why, it's not half the size of the snowballs I made when I was a small bear.' He gave the snowball a push, to send it on its way down the path once more – but the snowball didn't move.

'Of course,' said Mr Manders, 'I didn't always make giant snowballs on my own. Sometimes there were two or three of us little bears. Or four or five,' he said, giving the snowball another push. 'In fact,' he said, 'there were lots of happy, laughing little bears.'

With a sigh, Edward James went to stand by Mr Manders, and together they pushed the snowball along the path, and down to the gap in the fence.

The field was full of thick, crisp snow, and the giant snowball went walloping over, and grew enormously on the first two turns.

'Were the snowballs as big as this?' asked Edward James, struggling along with the snow up to his knees.

'Oh, much bigger!' said Mr Manders.

Edward James and Mr Manders pushed the snowball into the middle of the field, then they lay back in the snow for a rest.

'Tell me about the laughing little bears,' said Edward James. But Mr Manders just folded his paws over his tummy, and went to sleep.

He slept contentedly for some time, then a cold north wind began to blow. Mr Manders woke, rubbed his paws together, and began to push the snowball. The snowball didn't move, for it was frozen to the ground. Mr Manders looked at it. 'I think it's time for lunch,' he said, and he and Edward James made their way back to the house, leaving the snowball alone in the field, with the two flat shapes of bears beside it.

When they returned, they saw Florence. She was standing by the gap in the fence, and looking at the snowball.

'I don't know what that is,' she said. 'But it's much too big.'

'It's a giant snowball,' said Edward James.

'Is it indeed,' said Florence, as she trotted off to the summer house.

'The trouble with small animals like Florence', said Mr Manders, 'is, that they don't understand. They don't understand how you can start by making just an ordinary giant snowball, and end by making the biggest giant snowball in the world.'

He leaned against the snowball, and pushed as hard as he could – but the snowball didn't move. He took some steps away from it, and ran at it, and kicked it – and still it didn't move. Then he leaned his back against it, and tried to walk backwards, but his paws just slipped on the snow, and he fell down with a thump.

'What we need is something we can use as a lever,' he said.

So Edward James went to the summer house, and borrowed the pole which Florence used to hold up the washing line. When he returned, Mr Manders prodded the pole round the base of the snowball.

At first, nothing happened. But after a while they heard the sound of cracking ice, and slowly the snowball began to move. Mr Manders and Edward James pushed the snowball right across the field. Then Mr Manders opened the gate, and with a mighty heave, pushed the snowball out into the lane.

'Where are we going?' asked Edward James. But Mr Manders seemed not to care where he

and the giant snowball went. On he plodded, puffing and grunting. Sometimes he stopped for a moment, and said 'Biggest . . . !' And sometimes he stopped and said, 'In the world!' Then on he went until he reached the place where the lane dipped down.

With a rumbling sound, like the sound of thunder, the giant snowball began to roll away. Faster and faster it went, leaving Mr Manders and Edward James behind. When it reached the bend in the lane, it stopped for a moment; then it disappeared.

Mr Manders and Edward James ran after the snowball; but when they turned the bend in the lane, all they found was a heap of snow lying at the foot of a tree. The giant snowball was no more.

For a time, Mr Manders and Edward James just stood and gazed – then Edward James said, 'Let's make a snowman!'

And Mr Manders said, 'Yes – why not!'

Spring-cleaning

Early one morning, Mr Manders was surprised to see Florence coming down the path which led to the house. She was carrying a broom and a dustpan, half a dozen yellow dusters and a large tin of polish. As she came closer, Mr Manders saw that her head was covered with a little checked scarf.

'Edward James,' said Mr Manders, 'I think we are going to be spring-cleaned. But,' he added firmly, 'I don't want to be spring-cleaned, and I won't be spring-cleaned!' He got up from the breakfast table, and sat down in his armchair.

The next moment, Florence came into the kitchen. 'Spring-cleaning time, Mr Manders!' she said.

Mr Manders and Edward James went for a long walk round the field. 'Sometimes it's hard to say "No",' said Mr Manders.

'Say, "No, but-thank-you-very-much-all-the-same," ' said Edward James.

'It doesn't make any difference,' said Mr Manders. 'Not if someone really wants to do something for you.'

They went round the field once more, and when they returned to the garden, they found that the carpet had been cleaned and hung on the washing line. There was a bright pattern of roses on the carpet that both Mr Manders and Edward James had forgotten about. Leaning against the back door was a picture of Mr Manders's ancestor – Darcy Manders, the bold balloonist. The glass of the picture had been cleaned, and the piercing glance of Darcy Manders's blue eyes could be clearly seen. He seemed to look straight at Mr Manders with a look that said, 'What a boring old bear you are!'

Mr Manders sighed. 'I hate spring-cleaning,' he said. 'It makes things *uncomfortably* clean.'

Then they went into the kitchen, and saw that the dresser had been pushed away from the wall, and that Florence was standing behind it.

Mr Manders was alarmed. His dresser had always stood against the far wall. He liked it standing against the far wall. But Florence said, 'I think your dresser would look much better against the other wall. Kindly come and help me, Mr Manders.'

So Mr Manders stood behind the dresser with Florence and began to push. But the dresser didn't move, for the little iron castors were stuck with rust and dust.

'Mr Manders,' said Florence, 'I think you should clean the castors.'

She handed him a stiff-bristled brush, and then she sat on the armchair, with Edward James, and watched as Mr Manders cleaned the castors. When all the rust and dust had been swept away, Mr Manders and Florence went behind the dresser, and began to push once more.

'Mr Manders,' said Florence, when still the dresser refused to move, 'I think you should oil the castors.'

So Mr Manders went to the shed, and got the oil can, and knelt down by the dresser. This is very silly, he said to himself, as he oiled each castor in turn. Why am I helping someone to do something that I don't want them to do? That is, move my dresser to a place where I don't want it to be.

It was a very interesting question, and he sat down on the floor to think about it. As he did so, Florence pushed the dresser across the kitchen floor.

Mr Manders got up and went out into the garden. As he went, he thought about his dresser, and of how it had always stood against the wall. It had always been the first thing he saw when he opened the kitchen door. Now he would see nothing but the blank wall, where the dresser used to be. 'But it's *my* dresser,' he said to himself. 'And – come to that – my wall.'

He felt much better after he had said this, so he said it again. 'My dresser! My wall!' he shouted. Then he turned about sharply, and marched back to the kitchen.

He found the dresser in its new place; but Florence was standing behind it, and pushing for all she was worth. 'It looked better on the other side, after all,' she said. Mr Manders went to help her.

'Of course, I knew that all the time,' he said – but Florence didn't seem to hear.

When the dresser was back in its place, Florence gathered up her broom and dustpan, her dusters and her tin of polish. 'I'll be back again next spring,' she said, as she trotted off to the summer house.

Mr Manders and Edward James looked at one another.

'It's a long time 'til next spring,' said Edward James.

'A very long time,' said Mr Manders. Then together they went for one last walk round the field. They left the door of the house wide open. When they came back there was a fine film of dust on the dresser. The smell of polish had faded, and everything was just as it had always been – except for the dazzling colours of the carpet, and the dreadful gleam in Darcy Manders's eye.

The Barometer

One day, Mr Manders decided that he would clear out the attic. He had often thought of doing this but somehow, as soon as he opened the attic door, he always thought of something else that he should be doing. Something more important than clearing out the attic. 'But today,' he said, 'absolutely nothing at all will stop me!'

He marched up the stairs with Edward James, threw open the door, and began at once to unwrap the bundles and boxes to see what was inside them, and if it was something worth keeping.

The very first box he opened was full of nightshirts with matching caps. They had belonged to Mr Manders's grandfather, and after looking at them carefully, Mr Manders decided that he would keep them for when he was a cold, old bear and needed a cap and shirt to keep him warm at night.

The thought of being a cold, old bear made him feel rather sad; but what he found in the next box cheered him up at once. It was a barometer in a beautiful polished wood case. It had a dial like the face of a clock. But instead of telling the time, it told what the weather would be like; cloudy, fair, wet, very wet, dry, very dry, thundery, showery, hot, very hot, cold, or very cold.

Mr Manders was very pleased. He hurried down the stairs, and into the hall to find the best place to hang the barometer.

'You see, Edward James,' he said, as he hammered a large nail into the wall, 'what you do is this – you come down in the morning, and you tap your barometer and find out what the weather is going to be like. Then you can make your plans, without the risk of getting wet, or too hot. Or even', he said, 'of getting too hot and *then* getting wet – on account of being caught in a summer thunderstorm.'

He hung the barometer on the nail, and tapped the glass. The needle swung round and pointed to 'Hot'. Mr Manders tapped the glass again and the needle moved to 'Very Hot'. Mr Manders sighed.

'It's impossible to clear out the attic on a very hot day,' he said. 'The only thing to do is to go across the field, find a shady spot and have a snooze.'

Edward James was surprised. Mr Manders had always been able to tell what the weather would be like. He just stood at the door and looked at the sky, sniffed the air a little, and then said whether it would be hot or cold, wet or dry.

'But that is the best thing about this wonderful invention,' said Mr Manders, 'it saves all the bother of looking and sniffing.' And without glancing once at the dark grey sky, he went over the garden, with Edward James at his side.

When they reached the gap in the fence they met Florence. She was wrapped up in her cloak, and she carried her umbrella with the duck's head handle. Mr Manders laughed when he saw her.

'You won't need that,' he said. 'The barometer says that it's going to be very hot.'

'Is it indeed,' said Florence, as she trotted along the side of the hedgerow.

'Poor Florence,' said Mr Manders in a kindly way. 'One always feels so foolish carrying a large umbrella on a very hot day.'

They reached the far side of the field and he lay down, folded his paws over his tummy, and went to sleep. Edward James sat and looked up at the clouds. They were growing darker and heavier, and the sky seemed to have sunk so low that it lay on the top of the hawthorn hedge.

Mr Manders was surprised when it began to rain. He and Edward James ran back to the house as fast as they could, and sat by the kitchen stove to dry. 'Perhaps there's a special way of tapping the barometer,' said Mr Manders. 'Perhaps I tapped it too hard.'

The next morning, when Mr Manders came downstairs, he gave the barometer a light tap with his paw. The needle circled round and stopped at 'Wet'. Then it moved a little further and pointed to 'Very Windy'.

Mr Manders closed all the doors and windows of the house, then stood looking out over the garden, waiting for the clouds to gather in the bright blue sky. 'I'm glad we have a barometer,' he said. 'Without it we should not have known that it was going to be wet and windy today. That is,' he added, 'not until we got wet, and the wind blew us over.'

As he spoke, he saw Florence making her way from the summer house wearing a large shady hat. Mr Manders and Edward James hurried out after her. 'It's going to be wet!' shouted Mr Manders. 'It's going to be very windy!' But Florence had disappeared through the gap in the fence. When Mr Manders and Edward James reached the field they could see nothing but the long grass, each blade standing still in the warm summer air.

'It's a very sad thing,' said Mr Manders as he ran across the field, 'a very sad thing indeed, to think of a small animal like Florence being blown about by the wind!'

'Tossed this way and that – like a paper bag!' he cried, as he parted the stalks of grass with his paws, and peered about.

But when at last they found Florence, she was not at all like a paper bag tossed in the wind. She was, in fact, sitting quite still and content in the middle of the field, crocheting a small lace collar.

'Very wet . . . ,' said Mr Manders, as he sat down by her side. 'Very windy . . . . The barometer says so!'

'Mr Manders,' said Florence, 'you shouldn't take too much notice of *things*. Sometimes a nose is better.'

So Mr Manders snuffed the air – and he could smell nothing but the scents of a long summer day.

The next morning when Mr Manders tapped the barometer, the needle pointed firmly to 'Very Dry'. But Mr Manders opened the door and looked up at the sky. It was a pale grey, and on the far side of the field he could see the darker clouds building themselves into a bank – a great wall of rain cloud which would soon drift over the garden, and burst.

Mr Manders sniffed the air once or twice, just to make sure before closing the door. Then, as there is little to do on a rainy day, he and Edward James climbed the stairs, and began to clear out the attic.

A Letter from Wilkins

One morning, Mr Manders got a letter. 'Dear old friend!' it said, 'I shall come to see you on the twenty-third. How pleasant it will be to talk about all the adventures we had together in the good old days. How well I remember them! Your old friend, Wilkins.'

'Wilkins?' said Mr Manders. 'I don't remember a Wilkins – and what were the adventures we had together?'

It was all very puzzling – and a little alarming. If I've forgotten Wilkins, thought Mr Manders, I might have forgotten other things – wonderful exciting things. And if I've forgotten them, why they might as well not have happened at all!

He trotted off to the end of the field, sat down

beneath the hedge and tried to remember as many things as he could. He could remember the arrival of Florence, and he could remember the spring-cleaning. And he could remember the trip in the hot air balloon as clearly as though it happened only yesterday.

He felt a little better after remembering all these things, so he lay down, folded his paws over his tummy and went to sleep.

He awoke at lunch time, and went back to the house. There on the mat was another letter from Wilkins. 'Are there any mountains nearby?' it said. 'How grand it would be to climb a mountain together again. Get out your climbing boots and your strong rope. Your old friend, Wilkins.'

Mountains, thought Mr Manders, as he trotted off over the field once more. It's very worrying to think that I might have forgotten a mountain – it's such a big thing to forget. He sat down, and put his chin in his paw. After a while, Edward James came and sat by his side.

'Tell me about Wilkins and the mountains!' he said. He was very proud to think that Mr Manders had been so bold as to climb a mountain, and he gazed at him with round shining eyes.

So Mr Manders tried to imagine what the mountain might have looked like. It would have been very tall, he thought. There would have been snow on the top or perhaps the top was hidden in a mist and couldn't be seen at all. Then he tried to imagine what it would have felt like to climb the mountain: how the craggy rocks felt under his paws, how the loose stones went hurtling down behind him, and how he would have fallen but for Wilkins, who held him fast on the end of the rope.

'Oh, magnificent Wilkins!' he cried, jumping up, and striding over the field as he told this story to Edward James. 'Out I swung – over the abyss!'

'Over the what!' cried Edward James – who was very excited by this story.

'A very deep bit,' said Mr Manders.

He lay down on the grass, for he felt a little tired after telling this story, and he was just about to take another nap, when Edward James said, 'Have you remembered it right? Perhaps it was *you* who saved *Wilkins*.'

Mr Manders sat up and looked at Edward James. 'Perhaps you're right,' he said. So he closed his eyes and tried to imagine what it would have been like: how he had clambered over the rocks with Wilkins far below him, how the rope round his waist had gone suddenly taut and how he had looked back, to see Wilkins swinging out over the abyss.

'What happened next?' cried Edward James.

But Mr Manders could remember no more, no matter how hard he tried. For there was, he told himself sadly, nothing to remember.

'It never really happened, Edward James,' he said. 'I just imagined it all.'

They went back to the house and Mr Manders wrote a letter to Wilkins. 'I have been up in a hot air balloon,' he wrote slowly, and a little regretfully. 'But I have never climbed a mountain.'

Mr Manders and Edward James went to post the letter. On the way back, Mr Manders suddenly remembered what Wilkins looked like. 'He is a tall, rather stoutish bear,' he told Edward James.

The next morning, Mr Manders found a postcard lying on the door mat. 'Quite right,' it said. 'It wasn't you – it was good old Bickers!' The postcard was signed 'Wilkins', and there was a P.S. 'Sorry, but must cancel visit.'

Mr Manders propped the postcard up on the mantelpiece, and went out into the garden with Edward James. I wish it *had* been me, he thought as he went. I could have told the story on winter nights. Edward James would have been so proud of me.

'It's just that some bears climb mountains,' he said aloud, 'and some don't.'

But Edward James wasn't listening. He was

imagining that he and Mr Manders were climbing
a mountain – up and up they went, and they had
almost reached the top when Mr Manders fell.
But Edward James held him fast on the end of
the rope.

'Out he swung,' said Edward James to himself
in a thrilling whisper. 'Out over the deep bit.
Over the abyss!'

The Surprise

One morning, when Mr Manders went out into the garden, he found Florence kneeling under the kitchen window, digging up a little patch of earth. 'What are you planting?' he asked.

'It's a surprise,' said Florence.

'A surprise?' said Mr Manders. 'It isn't a snap-dragon, is it?'

'Indeed it is not!' said Florence, and she got up, brushed the earth from her apron, and trotted off back to the summer house.

Mr Manders went back to the kitchen, where Edward James was eating his breakfast. 'I don't really care much for surprises,' said Mr Manders, 'especially surprises in the garden. I like to know what will grow, and what it will look like.'

'Perhaps Florence has left the seed packet in the garden,' said Edward James. 'If you found the seed packet, you could read the name of the plant.'

Mr Manders didn't think that Florence would leave the seed packet in the garden, for she was a tidy little animal. But it might have fallen out of her apron pocket. So he went outside, and looked carefully along the path. The seed packet was nowhere to be seen.

'Perhaps the wind's blown it over the garden,' said Edward James.

So Mr Manders looked in his garden – then he looked in Florence's garden – then he lifted the lid of her dustbin, and looked inside.

There was nothing at all in the dustbin, except a scrap of paper lying at the bottom. There were some words printed on the paper. Mr Manders leant over the bin to try to read them – and he had just made out the letter 'B', when Florence came from the summer house, and slammed the door.

Mr Manders was startled. He swayed this way and that on the edge of the bin – and then he fell in head first, with his paws in the air.

Edward James came running down the path, and together he and Florence pushed the dustbin on to its side. Mr Manders scrambled out.

'What were you doing in my dustbin, Mr Manders?' asked Florence.

'Nothing,' said Mr Manders, and he turned and trotted off back to the house.

At first he felt a little foolish – but after a while, he stopped feeling foolish, and began to feel angry. After all, he told himself, a bear has the *right* to know what has been planted in his own garden. He opened the door, and strode off down the path, to where Edward James and Florence stood by the summer house. As he went, he planned what he would say. He would say, 'Kindly inform me, what manner of plant has been planted in my garden!' Or, perhaps, 'What manner of plant has been planted in my garden, kindly inform me!'

Then he reached Florence's side, made her a deep bow, and said, 'Kindly plant me. What manner of plant!'

'Mr Manders,' sid Florence, 'why is there a bus ticket stuck on the top of your head?'

Mr Manders went back to the house, and closed the door.

Early next morning, he crept out, and knelt beside the little patch of newly dug earth. He felt about very gently, until he found the seed. It was quite a large seed, and he was sitting there with it in his paw when Florence came up behind him.

'Put that back at once!' she said.

Mr Manders put the seed back in the earth. 'I just want to know what kind of a plant it will be,' he said.

'I have no intention of telling you,' said Florence. 'It will spoil the surprise.'

There was nothing else to do but wait until the seed grew into a plant. But what kind of a plant? Mr Manders couldn't go to sleep for wondering about it. Would it be a flower? A herb? A bush? A tree? Or would it be something he had never thought of before – a giant marrow!

'I feel certain that is what it will be,' said Mr Manders. He wasn't sure he liked the idea of a giant marrow lying under his kitchen window. 'But at least I know what it is,' he said to Edward James.

But when at last the seedling appeared, it didn't look at all like the start of a giant marrow. Day after day it grew, until it could be seen from the kitchen window – then it grew until its leaves almost covered the window panes, and the kitchen was filled with a lovely dim, green light.

At last the plant grew so tall that it was almost as high as the house. A great yellow flower had opened at the top of the stalk – and, little by little, as the day wore on, it turned so that it always faced the sun.

'Well?' said Florence. 'Do you like your sunflower, Mr Manders? Do you like your surprise?'

But Mr Manders could only nod; for every time he looked at his sunflower, he was overcome with delight. So, instead of saying 'thank you' he crept down to Florence's garden, in the dead of night, and planted some begonias – as a surprise.

Poskitt

Early one morning, Florence knocked on Mr Manders's door. 'My nephew, Poskitt is spending the day with me,' she said. 'I thought it only polite to inform you.'

Mr Manders was alarmed. He had heard of nephews – they were the sons of one's brother or sister, and they were usually very young, very noisy and full of mischief. 'Is he a *good* nephew?' asked Mr Manders.

'He is a very *small* nephew,' said Florence firmly. And with that she trotted back to the summer house.

Mr Manders went out into the garden and listened. All was quiet. 'Good,' he said – for he had decided to spend a peaceful day, just sitting and thinking of all the jobs which he would do tomorrow – or perhaps the day after that.

But he had scarcely settled himself on the doorstep, when he was startled by a loud cry of 'Poskitt! Come down at once!'

Mr Manders and Edward James hurried to where Florence stood gazing up into a tree. Mr Manders and Edward James looked up, but could see only leaves and branches. Edward James thought that he saw two bright eyes and the tip of a bushy tail – but he wasn't sure.

'He must be a very small nephew indeed!' said Mr Manders.

'He is a very *young* nephew,' said Florence. And with that she went back into her house and closed the door.

Mr Manders decided that instead of sitting on
the doorstep, he would spend his peaceful day
under the tree. But he had scarcely settled his
back against the trunk when he was struck on the
head by a conker.

Mr Manders was rather annoyed. He put the
conker in his pocket, and climbed the tree. He
climbed very slowly, with Edward James behind
him. Up and up they went, until they nearly
reached the top. Poskitt was nowhere to be seen,
but the view was wonderful. So Mr Manders
thought that he would spend his day sitting
on a branch.

'It's so peaceful here,' he said to Edward
James. 'And there's so much to see; the field, the
house, the garden.'

'And a big black hole,' said Edward James.

'Big black hole?' said Mr Manders. He scrambled down from the tree and ran across the garden. Sure enough, there it was – a big black hole in the middle of his lawn. Mr Manders went to the edge of the hole and looked inside. But there was little to be seen except for some worms, who had poked their heads out from the side of the hole and looked rather bewildered.

Mr Manders and Edward James followed the row of muddy footprints which led down the garden path and through the gap in the fence. But once they reached the gap in the fence, the footprints disappeared.

Mr Manders stood for a while and listened. All was still and quiet. So he decided that he would spend the rest of the day lying peacefully in the warm grass. He lay on his back, and closed his eyes – and he was almost asleep when he was startled by loud cries of WHEEEE! and YIPEEE! and HURRAH!

Yipee . . . thought Mr Manders. Hurrah? And
he raised his head in time to see a party of
fieldmice come hurtling through the grass, over
his portly stomach and down the other side.
Amongst the group of mice was one who did not
look quite like the others, but the whole party
moved so quickly that Mr Manders couldn't be
sure if it was Poskitt or not. He got up, plodded
over the field and sat down beneath the hedge.

'This whole business has made me feel very tired,' he said to Edward James. He made himself comfortable, and closed his eyes – and he was almost asleep when he was startled by a loud cry of 'POOOOOSKITT!'

Mr Manders jumped to his feet, and a moment later Florence came hurrying through the long grass towards him. 'It's almost time for tea,' she said. 'Kindly help me find Poskitt, Mr Manders.'

So for the rest of the afternoon, Mr Manders and Edward James wandered about the field. 'I shall be very glad to meet young Poskitt,' said Mr Manders. 'I have one or two things to say to him.' But Poskitt was nowhere to be seen.

From time to time Mr Manders or Edward James heard a rustling in the grass, and cried 'Ha-ha!' But they only managed to discover one another, and muttered 'Oh, it's you', feeling very foolish indeed.

The sun began to go down, the light grew dim, and as there was nothing else to be done they made their way back to the house. There, sitting on the doorstep, was Poskitt.

He was very small, very young and very muddy. He looked exactly like Florence, and in his dirty little paw he held a big bunch of begonias. 'For you!' he said to Mr Manders. 'Thankyouverymuchforalovelytime!' And before Mr Manders could say anything at all, he scurried off down the path.

Mr Manders went into the kitchen and put the flowers in a jar. 'It's been an odd sort of day,' he said to Edward James. 'I've been hit on the head, there's a hole in my lawn, I've been mistaken for a small hill and given a bunch of my *own* begonias!'

He sat down in his armchair and folded his paws over his tummy. 'But some days are just *like* that,' he said.

A Puzzling Question

One evening, when Edward James was sitting in the kitchen, he suddenly thought, where was I, before I was living in this house with Mr Manders? He went to find Mr Manders to ask him.

Mr Manders was planting begonias in a flowerbed.

'Where was I, before I was here?' asked Edward James.

'You were sitting in the kitchen,' said Mr Manders.

'Where was I *before* I was sitting in the kitchen?' said Edward James. 'Before my breakfast – before *anything*!'

Mr Manders said that he didn't know. He

found Edward James's question very puzzling, and he went for a walk by himself to think about it. He walked right across the field, but he couldn't remember a time when Edward James hadn't been there.

Mr Manders went back to the kitchen. 'Think hard, Edward James,' he said. 'Try to remember where you were before you were here.'

Edward James thought very hard. He thought that he could remember last Tuesday, he said, but he wasn't sure.

'Try harder,' said Mr Manders. So Edward James tried harder – and he did remember last Tuesday.

'I was here,' he said. 'Where was I before that?'

Mr Manders got out a pad and a pencil, and he and Edward James sat down at the kitchen table. 'The thing to do,' he said, 'is to write everything down when we remember it. Then we won't forget it again. And we'll start at the beginning. When did we meet?'

Edward James said that he couldn't remember.

'Neither can I,' said Mr Manders.

They left the pad and the pencil on the table, and went out into the garden. Where *was* Edward James before he was here, thought Mr Manders. And then he thought, where was *I* before I was here? He thought as hard as he could – but he couldn't remember. Faster and faster he walked, as he tried to remember the mysterious time before he had lived with Edward James in the house by the stream.

'Why can't I remember it?' he said, as he went round and round, with Edward James trotting behind him. It was like trying to remember where he had put his gloves – sometimes he almost had the answer, and then he lost it again.

'Where *was* I!' he shouted, holding up his paws to the night sky. Then he looked at his paws, and turned them this way and that. They were a bit battered, and the velvet had worn thin in places. They are old paws, thought Mr Manders, but they are still good paws.

'I have been here a long time,' he said to Edward James. 'So much has happened to me that I can't remember it.' Then he looked at Edward James's paw. It was small and new, and firmly stuffed. 'But you haven't been here a long time,' he said. 'So you haven't got a lot to remember.'

But Edward James still wanted to know the answer to his question, and he stood in the field, staring at Mr Manders.

'I don't know,' said Mr. Manders. 'I can't remember how we met – or anything.'

He took Edward James's paw, and led him back over the field and through the gap in the fence. 'But we *did* meet,' he said, 'and that's the most important thing.'

They went down the path in silence. The kitchen door stood open, and the flames that burned in the little iron stove shone brightly, and lit up the room. It looked warm and welcoming. 'I think we were here,' said Mr Manders. 'I think we have always been here.'

'Will we be here forever?' said Edward James.

'I expect so,' said Mr Manders.